W9-AXZ-569

and the New Kid

NANCY CARLSON

VIKING

VIKING

Published by the Penguin Group
Viking Penguin, a division of Penguin Books USA Inc.,
375 Hudson Street, New York, New York 10014, U.S.A.
Penguin Books Ltd, 27 Wrights Lane, London W8 5TZ, England
Penguin Books Australia Ltd, Ringwood, Victoria, Australia
Penguin Books Canada Ltd, 10 Alcorn Avenue, Toronto, Ontario, Canada M4V 3B2
Penguin Books (N.Z.) Ltd, 182–190 Wairu Road, Auckland 10, New Zealand

Penguin Books Ltd, Registered Offices: Harmondsworth, Middlesex, England

First published in 1990 by Viking Penguin, a division of Penguin Books USA Inc.
3 5 7 9 10 8 6 4
Copyright © Nancy Carlson, 1990
All rights reserved

ISBN 0-670-82499-2
Library of Congress Catalog Card number 89-24841
CIP data available upon request

Printed in Japan
Set in Clarendon Book

For Barry...
who, just like Arnie,
teased someone and learned his lesson.

There was a new kid in school named Philip.

Philip was different from most kids.
He needed help doing some things.

Other times he didn't need any help at all.

Philip didn't have many friends at school.

No one knew how to play with a boy
in a wheelchair.

At recess Arnie would yell, "Let's race Philip!"
Of course Arnie would always win.

Arnie would tease Philip.
"Boy, do you eat slow," said Arnie.

One day after school Arnie started to tease Philip,
"Hey, look at me, I'm Philip!"

But Arnie didn't watch where
he was going.

"Ouch," cried Arnie.

"Call the nurse!" yelled Philip.

Arnie was rushed to the hospital!

A week later, Arnie came back to school.
He had a broken leg, a twisted wrist,
and a sprained tail!
Arnie needed help carrying his books.
It took him a long time to get anywhere.

At lunch, Tina had to get Arnie his food.
Arnie ate real slow. "It's hard to eat peas with
my left hand," complained Arnie.
Even Philip finished his lunch before Arnie.

During gym class Philip challenged
Arnie to a race. Philip won!

"Let me help you up, Arnie," said Philip.
"Boy, I could use a wheelchair like you!" said Arnie.

After school Arnie discovered Philip had
a huge baseball card collection.
Philip asked Arnie over to his house.
"Well, I don't know. What will we do?" asked Arnie.
"You'll see," said Philip.

Arnie had a ball at Philip's.
They played computer games all afternoon.

Soon Arnie and Philip were doing everything together.

After a few weeks Arnie got his cast off.
Arnie was so happy.

During lunch, Arnie ate so fast that Philip didn't get a chance to talk to him.

After school Tina asked Arnie to play ball.
Arnie said, "On one condition...

"…as long as I can bring my coach."
"Sure!" said Tina.
And they all went to play baseball.

DATE DUE			
SEP 20 '93			